The Girl and her Dragons

Written by Suzanne Ridgway
Illustrated by Imogen Ridgway (Aged 8 ½)

To Imogen (the girl with the dragons),

This book is for you because your imagination sparked mine.

I'm so proud of you.

Love,
Mummy
x

Issy has always had dragons - friendly ones! Ever since she was old enough to tell her mum about them. They come and go. Sometimes they stay for a while; sometimes they go for a while. But what matters most is that they are always there when Issy needs them.

The important thing to know is that only Issy can see these magical creatures. They are created from her imagination and dreamt up to be whatever she wants them to be.

For Issy, they are very real indeed.

Issy is a very happy little girl.

She's always smiling and laughing and she is very funny. She's incredibly kind and thoughtful and has the biggest heart of anyone you'll ever know.

Issy's beautiful. She has glossy red hair and big chocolate brown, sparkly eyes.

Everybody loves Issy.

Issy was three when a dragon first arrived in her life. One sunny afternoon, she spotted a dragon sat on the roof of her car.

"Drive carefully, Mummy! He might fall off!"

Surprised at first, Issy's mum soon became used to having a dragon pop up at unexpected times - at bedtime, at lunchtime, watching television, taking a bath...at any time day or night, there was always a chance Issy would announce that a dragon had appeared.

It wasn't until Issy was six years old that she finally gave her dragon a name.

One evening whilst in the bath, Issy was having so much fun that she was making some rather large puddles on the floor from all the splashing. She began to laugh.

"Are you okay in there, Issy?" shouted Mum from the bedroom.

"Yes! Just playing with Bathmatic"

"Bath-what?" said Mum.

"Bathmatic! My dragon!"

"Oh, the dragon! Silly me!" laughed Mum.

Soon, one dragon became a whole dragon family.

Bathmatic is dad to eight little dragons. With his two youngest dragons, Bob and John, they are the three who visit Issy the most.

When the dragons were babies, Issy could sit baby Bob in the palm of her hand. Now he's two, and growing every day, he couldn't possibly fit!

Bathmatic, who is dark blue with orange spikes, is the friendliest dragon you'd care to meet. He's quite big. He's bigger than Issy, but he's not a giant.

Issy and her dragons have lots of fun adventures together.

One year for Bathmatic's birthday, Issy arranged a tea party for all the dragons to help him celebrate.

Together with her mum, Issy spent the morning hanging pretty bunting and blowing up balloons. Mum set the table, making sure each dragon had a chair, a plate and a party hat. Issy poured the tea into little teacups and served Bathmatic's favourite - lemon cake.

The whole family sang Happy Birthday as Bathmatic blew out the candles on his cake. Except for one little dragon - Bob. After eating too many cheese sandwiches, he had sneaked upstairs, curled up on Issy's bed and fallen asleep!

Last year, the dragon family joined Issy on her first holiday abroad. When Issy told her mum that the dragons would be joining them, there was a little confusion as to how they'd get there.

Would they sit on top of the plane as they did the car? Would they fly alongside with Issy watching them through the window?

Issy said the dragons were flying to Paris first for a mini-holiday of their own. They wanted to visit the Eiffel Tower! They made sure to fly off before everyone else and made it to Greece just in time to see Issy's plane land. Phew!

They all had a such a fantastic holiday!

One day, Issy was lucky enough to join her mum on a visit to the local radio station. She was so excited!

The radio was looking for exciting stories to tell their listeners. Issy's mum had written to them to tell them a little bit about Issy's dragons. They wanted to meet Issy as soon as possible to find out more.

The radio presenter hit the big red button. Issy was live on air!

As Issy sat and talked about her dragons, she had the eyes of everyone in the room fixed on her, their mouths wide open in amazement. Everyone was entranced.

But of course, she wasn't alone. In between Issy and her mum was Bathmatic, sat tall with his chest out, a big smile on his face, so very proud of his little best friend.

When Issy was eight years old, she decided to take her dragons to school for the first time. It made the other children very curious indeed.

"You have dragons?"

"Are they real?"

"Are they friendly?"

"Do they breathe fire?"

Issy didn't know which question to answer first!

That night at bedtime, Issy told her mum about all the questions she had been asked in the playground. Some of the children even found it quite strange that she had dragons. It must have been a surprise, that's for sure!

Issy's mum settled down on the bed next to Issy.

"That is the great thing about imagination, Issy. It can take you to wherever you want to go, with whoever you want to go with.

Not everybody will understand because the dragons are yours. But I think you're a very clever little girl with a daring ability to dream."

"Thanks, Mummy" said Issy.

Now Issy is eight and a half years old and she has ten dragons!

Tomorrow, Issy will say goodbye to the dragons for a little while. Bathmatic and his family are going on a bike ride together. The dragons have a bike that's very long, with a seat for each dragon!

The dragons aren't always with Issy and when they leave, they have amazing adventures of their own. They'll wave their goodbyes and fly away.

But be prepared, because you never know when a dragon, or ten, might next pop up for some fun!

Never stop dreaming. For who knows what the next adventure could be...

THE END

The dragons:

Bathmatic	Dad
Abigail	Mum
Max	9 years old
Layla	8 years old
Joey	7 years old
Archie	7 years old
Bella	6 years old
Stella	5 years old
John	4 years old
Bob	2 years old

Printed in Great Britain
by Amazon